This book belongs to

_____

Note to parents and carers

Many children are now taught to read using the phonic approach. This means they are taught to look at the letters, say the sounds, and then blend them to make a word. So, for example, children blend **c/a/t** to make the word **cat**, and **sh/o/p** to make **shop**.

When children have completed their initial phonics learning, they are ready to apply it to reading real books. Ladybird's **Superhero Phonic Readers** are planned for this exciting stage.

Some words are hard to read using beginner phonics. These words are often known as 'tricky words'. Some of these occur frequently in the English language so it is useful for children to memorize them.

Have fun doing our Tricky Words Memory Quiz on page 30. This features the most useful tricky words from the story.

How to use Superhero Phonic Readers:

★ Start at level one and gradually progress through the series. Each story is a little bit longer than the last and uses more grown-up vocabulary.

★ Children will be able to read **Superhero Phonic Readers** for themselves. Let your child read to you, and share the excitement!

★ If your child finds any words difficult, help him or her to work out the sounds in the word.

★ Early readers can be concentrating so hard on the words that they sometimes don't fully grasp the overall meaning of what they read. The puzzle questions on pages 28 and 29 will help with this. Have fun talking about them together.

★ There is a reward chart at the back of the book - young readers can fill this in and add stickers to it.

★ The Ladybird website **www.ladybird.com** features a wealth of information about phonics and reading.

★ Enjoy reading together!

Geraldine Taylor
Ladybird Educational Consultant

Educational Consultant: Geraldine Taylor

Phonics Consultant: Marj Newbury

A catalogue record for this book is available from the British Library

Published by Ladybird Books Ltd
80 Strand, London, WC2R 0RL
A Penguin Company

2 4 6 8 10 9 7 5 3 1
© LADYBIRD BOOKS LTD MMIX
LADYBIRD and the device of a Ladybird are trademarks of Ladybird Books Ltd

ISBN: 978-1-40930-266-7

Printed in Italy

Superhero Phonic Readers

Stella Stone

written by Dick Crossley

illustrated by Deborah van de Leijgraaf

Every night, before she went to bed, Mrs Stone liked to look at the stars. One night, as she looked out from her bedroom window, a bright light suddenly shot across the sky.

"What was that odd light in the sky?" Mrs Stone
asked her husband, as they went to bed.
"A comet, I think," said Mr Stone.

As the Stones slept, the comet fell slowly from the sky…

…and landed in their back garden.

The next morning, Mr Stone took a good look at it.

"It's some sort of space rock!" he said.

Just then, there was a loud, cracking sound.

Mr Stone stood back as the rock split apart.

To the Stones' amazement, inside it was…

…a little girl!

"We will call her Stella," said Mrs Stone. "Stella Stone."

The Stones soon found that Stella was not like other children. Their little girl from the stars had a special gift. Stella was very, very strong.

In fact, she had the strength of ten men!

Stella's super-strength came in very handy.

She used it to help her mum.

She used it to help her dad.

And she used it to help lots of other people.

The Stone family were very happy.

But, far away on another planet, plans were being hatched.
Plans that might spoil the Stone family's happiness.
Stella's shell came from the planet Kronk.

Blobby green things called Kronkoids lived on Kronk.

They grew super-strong children in special rock shells.

When the children hatched, the Kronkoids made them work,
very hard, in Kronk's mines.

But Stella had been lucky. Before her shell hatched,
a blast had sent it flying across space.

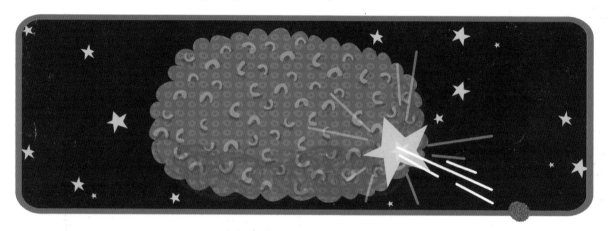

Now the Kronkoids had found out about Stella's escape.
They had tracked the path of her shell to Mr and Mrs Stone's
back garden. And they were setting off to bring Stella back.

Stella was helping her dad when the Kronkoid spaceship landed. She was surprised to see the green blobs slip down the ship's ramp.

The Kronkoids did not hang about. With a blast from their stun guns, they froze Mr Stone to the spot.

Then they took aim at Stella. But Stella was not going to give in without a fight. With a super-strong tug, she ripped up a strip of lawn.

The Kronkoids went flying. Splat!

The Kronkoids got up, and tried to attack Stella again.
This time, she tore up a tree, and clobbered them with it.
Thwack!

Again, the Kronkoids got up and slithered towards Stella. So Stella picked up the garden shed, and dropped it on top of them. Squish!

The Kronkoids gave up. They squeezed out from under the shed and slithered back up the ramp into their spaceship.

Stella had not finished yet.

She picked up the Kronkoid spaceship.
With all her super-strength, she hurled it into the sky
– back to where it came from.

By now, Mr Stone could move again. As he watched
the spaceship zoom away, he gave Stella a big hug.
"I don't think they will be back again in a hurry!" he said.

Mr Stone was right. The Kronkoids rushed back to their home planet. When the other children found out how Stella had got rid of them, they soon followed her example.

That night, Stella looked up at the stars from her bedroom window. She was very happy to be staying with her new family.

But she wished she had somebody else to play with, too.
"I wish I had a little brother," she said to herself.

Then she checked under her bed for monsters,

got in, and was soon fast asleep.

Later that night…

The next day…

Superhero Secret Puzzles

⭐ How did Stella arrive?

⭐ Where had she come from?

⭐ What was Stella's special gift?

⭐ How did she fight off the Kronkoids?

⭐ Do you think the little boy in the last picture will be super-strong, too?

⭐ If you had the strength of ten men, what would you do?

Look at these pictures from the story and say the order they should go in.

A

B

C

D

Answer on page 30.

Tricky Words Memory Quiz

Can you remember these words from the story?

See if you can read them super-fast.

she	said	when
to	Mr	work
Mrs	their	going
the	some	so
one	he	into
out	there	all
her	little	where
what	we	could
was	people	be
asked	were	
they	another	
I	called	

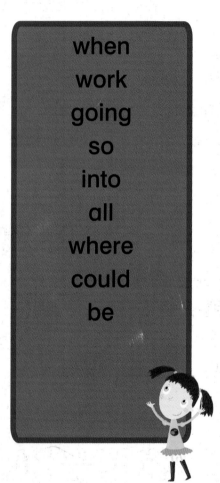

What else can you remember?

Can you put the book down and say what happens in the story?

The answer to the picture puzzle on page 29 is D, A, C, B.

I'm a phonic
Superhero

I can read all of *Stella Stone*.

I can read all the tricky words.

By _____

Date _____

level
9

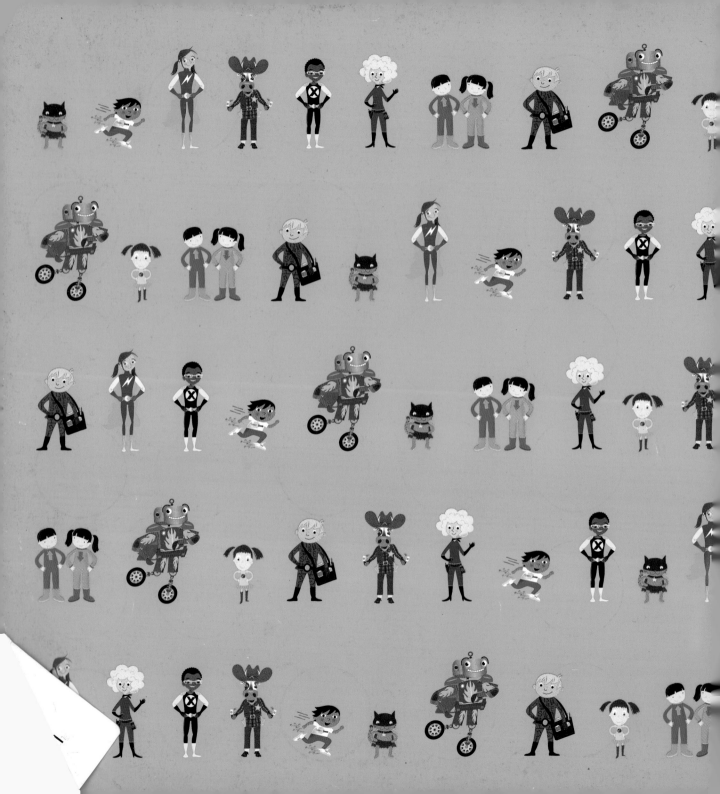